THE GROSS HUMAN BODY IN ACTION
AUGMENTED REALITY

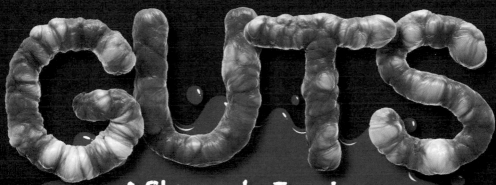

A Stomach-Turning
AUGMENTED REALITY
Experience

Percy Leed

Lerner Publications ◆ Minneapolis

EXPLORE THE HUMAN BODY IN BRAND-NEW WAYS WITH AUGMENTED REALITY!

1. Ask a parent or guardian for permission to download the free Lerner AR app on your digital device by going to the App Store or Google Play. When you launch the app, choose the Gross Human Body series.

2. As you read, look for this icon throughout the book. It means there is an augmented reality experience on that page!

3. Use the Lerner AR app to scan the picture near the icon.

4. Watch the human body's systems come alive with augmented reality!

CONTENTS

INTRODUCTION
THAT'S NASTY

What's that funny feeling coming from your gut? It could be a booming belch. Or maybe it's a stinky fart that's ready to burst.

Stomach pain can be caused by gas, rotten food, or other nasty things.

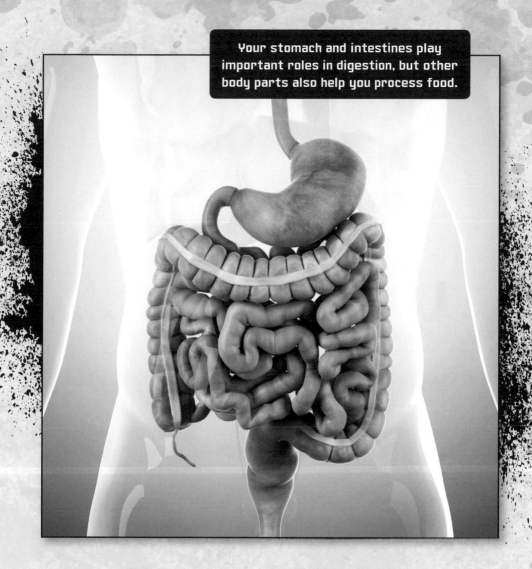

Your stomach and intestines play important roles in digestion, but other body parts also help you process food.

Digestion turns food into energy, water, and . . . poop. Chewed food arrives in the stomach. Think of your stomach as a big, wrinkled balloon with mucus and acid inside. When it's empty, it's barely big enough to hold a mouthful of water. But it can stretch to hold almost 1 gallon (3.8 L) of food. It turns out, all kinds of nasty things happen deep inside your belly.

ONE BIG ACID BATH: YOUR STOMACH

Acid can burn a hole through your skin. It can even chew through metal. So what part of your body makes almost 4 pints (1.7 L) of acid every day? Your stomach!

Your stomach squirts that acid all over itself to digest food such as cheeseburgers. It turns the cheese, pickles, and ketchup into vitamins and protein. Your stomach doesn't

The digestive process begins before you take your first bite of food.

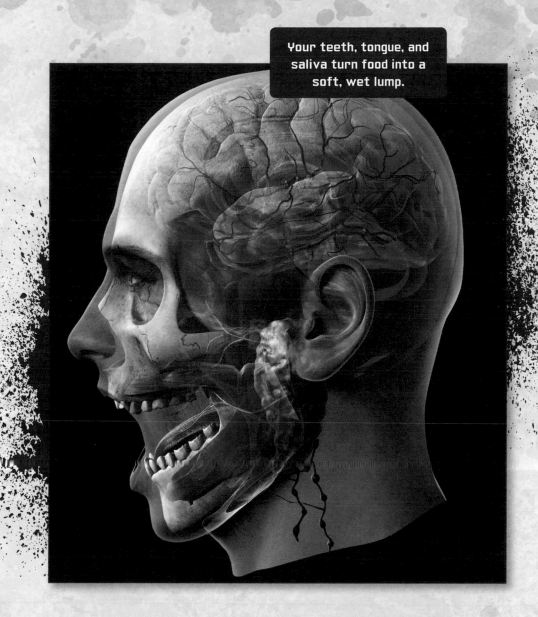

Your teeth, tongue, and saliva turn food into a soft, wet lump.

do that by itself. It's just one step in the digesting process. The whole slimy business begins before you even take a bite of food.

At the thought of food, your mouth begins to make saliva, or spit. Saliva softens food to help you swallow it. When

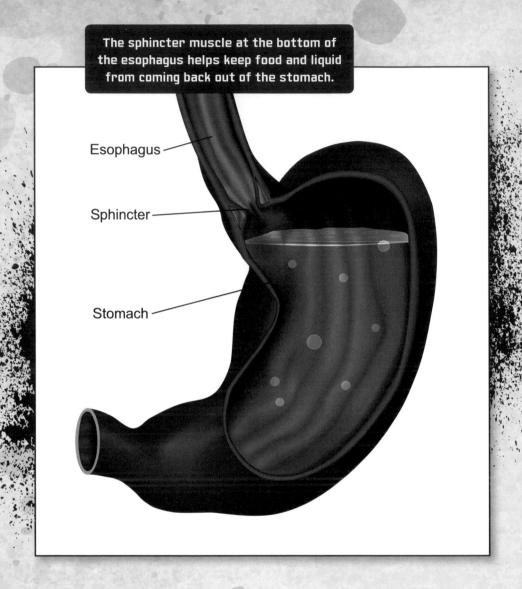

The sphincter muscle at the bottom of the esophagus helps keep food and liquid from coming back out of the stomach.

Esophagus

Sphincter

Stomach

you chew, your teeth grind food into a saliva-soaked paste. Mmm . . . delicious!

The food travels down your throat and through the esophagus. It passes the sphincter, a ring-shaped muscle. Once the food passes into the stomach, the muscle squeezes shut to keep food from coming back the other way.

The stomach's inner walls have thousands of rugae. These ripply flaps and folds let the stomach stretch when it's full of mashed-up food. And it gets worse! The rugae are full of tiny holes like mini squirt guns. They shoot stomach acid and other juices. The acidy juice breaks down food into chyme, a goopy mush. Once it is mushy enough, the chyme squirts into the small intestine.

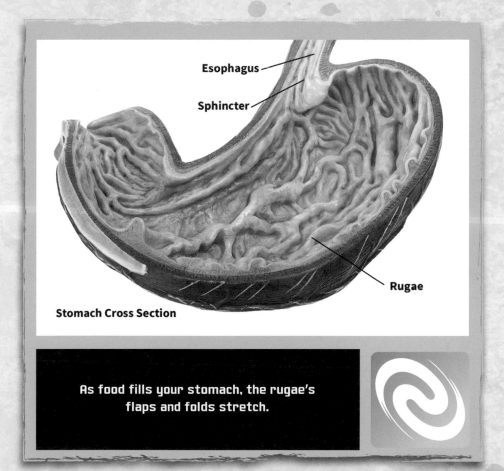

Esophagus

Sphincter

Rugae

Stomach Cross Section

As food fills your stomach, the rugae's flaps and folds stretch.

A thick layer of slimy mucus coats your stomach. The acid can't eat through the mucus, so the walls of your stomach are safe. What a relief!

Sometimes, stomach acid acts up. It might sneak into the esophagus. Have you ever felt a burning feeling at the bottom of your throat? That's stomach acid. The feeling is often called heartburn.

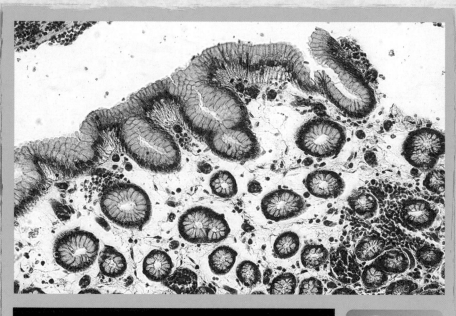

Rugae cells activate and begin squirting acid when food enters the stomach.

Helicobacter pylori bacteria in your stomach can make the mucus layer thin and lead to ulcers.

The mucus layer in the stomach can get too thin, letting acid get through. Then the acid attacks the stomach walls. Soon there's an open sore called an ulcer. Ugh.

WHAT GOES IN MUST COME OUT: ALL ABOUT POOP

Still not grossed out? Well, this next section just might send you running.

The chyme that leaves your stomach gets turned into poop. Poop is nasty. You might call it feces, fecal matter, waste, number two, or poop. It's basically a lump of everything your body wants to get rid of. Chyme from the stomach is

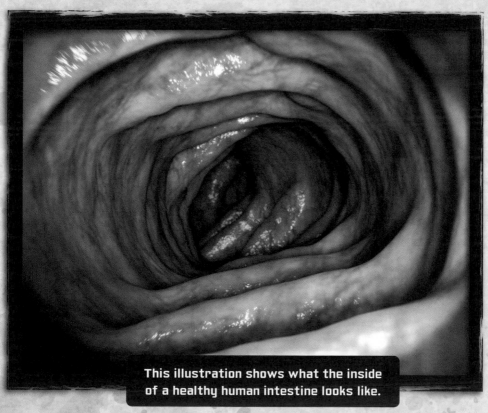

This illustration shows what the inside of a healthy human intestine looks like.

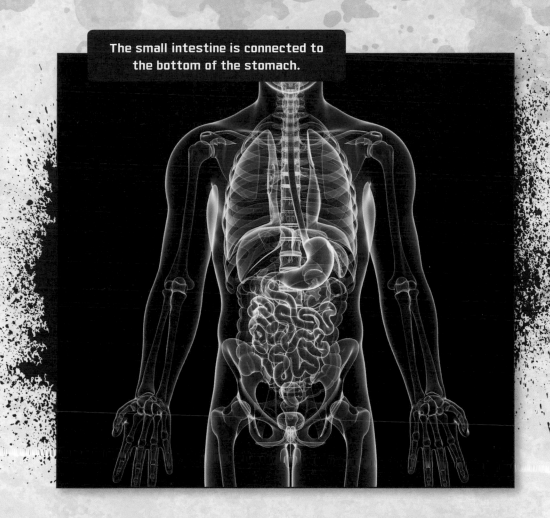

The small intestine is connected to the bottom of the stomach.

poop's star ingredient. The chyme has the look and feel—but definitely not the taste!—of melted ice cream. But before it gets turned into poop, it passes through both of your intestines.

The small intestine makes sure that every nutrient is squeezed out of the goop before it becomes poop. It has thousands of villi, tiny fingerlike bumps that stir up the chyme. They also take in nutrients and send them to the rest of the body.

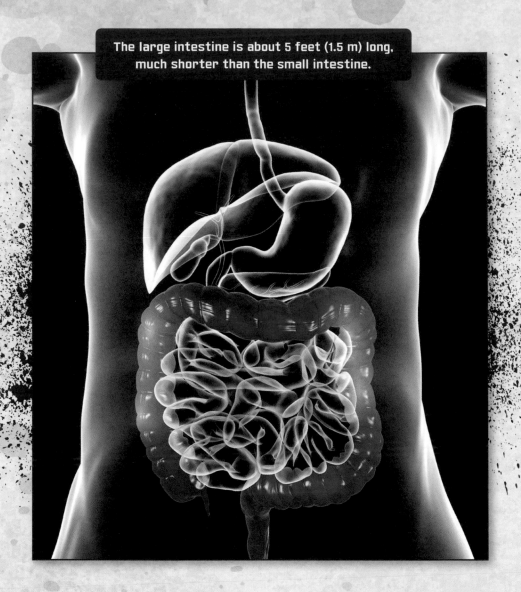

The large intestine is about 5 feet (1.5 m) long, much shorter than the small intestine.

In the large intestine, the melted-ice-cream-like goop becomes poop. First, the intestine gets rid of some of the chyme's water. The intestine absorbs the water. It adds used-up cells and other waste that are floating in your body. Then the goop is more like a mushy piece of poop.

Poop has one more stop before it's ready. Poop hangs out in the rectum until you deposit it into the toilet. When enough poop collects in the rectum, you'll feel the urge to go. On the toilet, your rectum muscles push the poop out. It exits through the anus. Most people poop one or two times a day.

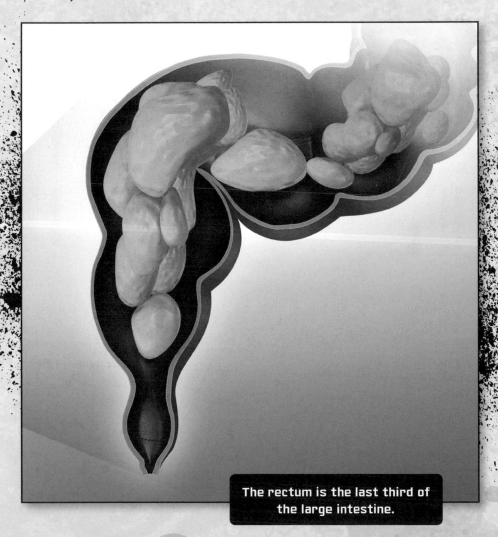

The rectum is the last third of the large intestine.

Do you wonder how much poop you poop? Most people poop about 1 ounce (28 g) of feces for each 12 pounds (5.4 kg) they weigh. So if you weigh 100 pounds (45 kg), you're probably dumping about half a pound (0.2 kg) of poop each time you go.

Poop can tell you a lot. If you eat a lot of meat, your poop pieces will probably be small and dark. If you eat lots of vegetables, you'll have more poop.

Milk, vegetables, and other foods have a big impact on what your poop looks like.

Have you ever eaten corn and then noticed undigested corn kernels in your poop later?

Some things—like corn—look almost the same coming out as they did going in. Got yellow poop? You've probably been drinking lots of milk. And if you eat beets, you may notice a reddish color to your turds.

GAS ATTACK: BELCHES AND FARTS

You're enjoying your lunch at school. You take a bite of your sandwich and a sip of your drink. Suddenly, you let out a loud *buuurp*. Once your body begins to burp, there's often nothing you can do to stop it. Sometimes, you just have to let it rip.

A burp is the result of gas getting trapped in your stomach.

Chugging soda pop is one of the best ways to produce a big, echoing belch.

A burp is gas escaping from your stomach. The air you breathe is full of gas such as oxygen. Every time you take a bite of food or a sip of a drink, you swallow a little air.

Swallowing air isn't the only way to trap gas in your stomach. Soda pop is full of the gas carbon dioxide. Every time you guzzle a soda, you get a bellyful of gas. But your stomach wants nothing to do with it. Back up it comes: *bra-a-a-a-ap!*

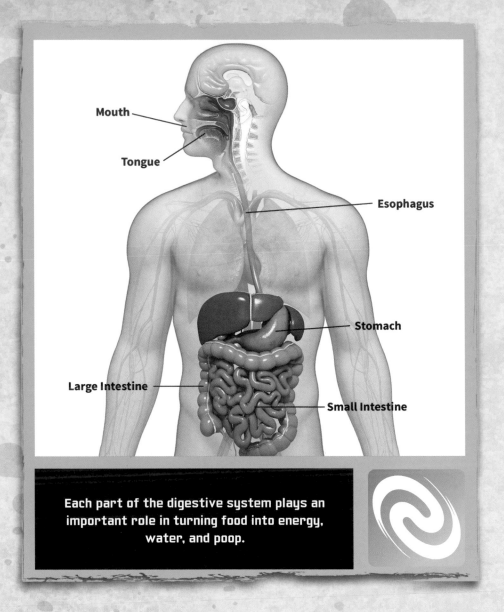

Mouth

Tongue

Esophagus

Stomach

Large Intestine

Small Intestine

Each part of the digestive system plays an important role in turning food into energy, water, and poop.

A loud, stinky fart is even more embarrassing than a big belch. But everybody farts. If gas makes it to the intestines, it comes out as a fart instead of a burp. Most farts are caused by swallowed air. These farts don't have much of an odor.

But we all know of another kind of toot: the silent but deadly fart. These quiet stink bombs are not caused by swallowed air. Instead, they're made when undigested food gets into the intestines.

The intestines are full of healthful bacteria. These bugs attack whatever food enters their home. They finish breaking down any remaining food into nutrients.

There's just one small side effect. As the bacteria attack the food, they create new gases. Stinky gases. And what do gases do when they get trapped in the intestines? They creep out, silent but deadly!

Of course, not all farts are equal. What you eat has a lot to do with the farts you make. Certain vegetables such as cauliflower and cabbage produce foul-smelling toots. Other stink producers are eggs, meat, and milk. If you want truly thunderous farts, eat lots of beans. Mix and match your foods, and you can brew some superfarts that are both loud and stinky!

CHAPTER 4

RUMBLING AND SPEWING: WHEN YOU GET SICK

Belches, farts, and poop are all perfectly natural. So what happens when things aren't going so smoothly? Rumbling in the stomach can cause spewing from two places.

Puking is one way your body protects itself from disease. Two things can make you sick enough to vomit.

Vomiting isn't fun, but if you feel sick, it can make you feel better—at least for a little while.

Rotavirus is a virus that can cause vomiting, fever, and other problems.

One is a virus. A virus is a tiny living thing that gets into your body and makes you sick. Your body vomits to get rid of the virus.

The other common cause of vomiting is food poisoning. Almost all food has some bacteria in it. Most bacteria are harmless. But sometimes your body takes in too much bad bacteria. Then it's time to hurl.

If you don't want to spend the rest of the day in the bathroom, avoid moldy foods. They're full of bad bacteria.

You won't have much time to find the bathroom. Your stomach muscles contract. They're pushing the food back out. The sphincter muscle at the top of the stomach opens. And then, well, let's just hope you made it to the bathroom in time.

Vomit comes in all sorts of shapes and colors. If you've eaten something with a strong color or smell, you may notice that in the vomit. Yuck!

Vomiting usually makes you feel a little better right away. But beware! You may get that yucky feeling again soon. Most people vomit more than once when they have a virus or food poisoning.

Even if you feel better after puking, it's a good idea to keep a bucket handy in case the sick feeling returns.

Diarrhea, or the runs, is when you have watery, runny poop. Your poop has gotten so runny that you can't keep it in. Diarrhea usually starts because you've eaten something bad. Or you may have an infection in your large intestine.

Diarrhea is sloppy and stinky. But it's just your body getting rid of unhealthy invaders such as bacteria. You often need more than one release of watery poop to feel healthy

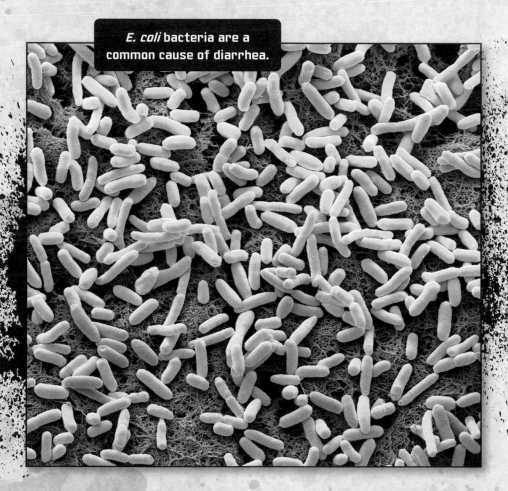

E. coli bacteria are a common cause of diarrhea.

Soon this burger will be wet, lumpy mush.

again. That's why, when you have the runs, you'll want to stick pretty close to a toilet.

Barfing and having the runs can really ruin your day. But as bad as they may seem at the time, they help your body get back to normal. Soon you'll feel better. Then your body can get back to the business of turning food into mush, belching, pooping, and farting!

- Borborygmi are growling and rumbling sounds your stomach makes. The sounds come from your stomach muscles digesting food.

- The average kid digests almost 1,000 pounds (453 kg) of food each year. In your lifetime, that could add up to more than 50 tons (45 t) of food.

- Your small intestine is only about 1 inch (2.5 cm) wide. But if it were stretched out end to end, it would be almost five times as tall as you.

- To keep poop moving, your large intestine coats itself in slimy mucus. The mucus allows the poop to glide right on through.

- On average, healthy people fart about fourteen times per day.

- People who puke too often can get rotten teeth from all that stomach acid gushing out of their mouths.

- On average, people get diarrhea about four times a year. Each time, the body dumps about 1 quart (0.9 L) of runny poop per day.

GLOSSARY

bacteria: tiny living things that live all around and inside you

chyme: mashed-up food that has already been digested by the stomach

digestion: breaking down food into smaller parts

esophagus: the tube that carries food from the throat to the stomach

feces: solid waste that leaves your body

infection: a sickness caused by a bacteria or virus

mucus: a thick, slippery liquid made by the body

nutrient: a substance that helps growth, provides energy, and maintains life

protein: a nutrient that helps build bones and muscles

rugae: ripply folds on the inside of the stomach

Biology for Kids: Bacteria
https://www.ducksters.com/science/bacteria.php

Digestive System
https://www.innerbody.com/image/digeov.html

Duhaime, Darla. *Gross Body Stuff*. Vero Beach, FL: Rourke, 2016.

Farndon, John. *Tiny Killers: When Bacteria and Viruses Attack*.
Minneapolis: Hungry Tomato, 2017.

Gross Science—How Far Do Sneezes and Vomit Travel?
https://wpt.pbslearningmedia.org/resource/nvgs-sci
-travellingsneezes/wgbh-nova-gross-science-how-far
-do-sneezes-and-vomit-travel/

Leed, Percy. *The Mouth (A Nauseating Augmented Reality Experience)*.
Minneapolis: Lerner Publications, 2021.

Settel, Joanne. *Your Amazing Digestion from Mouth through Intestine*.
New York: Atheneum, 2019.

Your Digestive System
https://kidshealth.org/en/kids/digestive-system.html

INDEX

PHOTO ACKNOWLEDGMENTS

Image credits: Goads Agency/Getty Images, p. 4; Eraxion/Getty Images, p. 5; Corina Marie Howell/Getty Images, p. 6; MedicalRF.com/Getty Images, p. 7; Medicalstocks/Getty Images, p. 8; Ben-Schonewille/Getty Images, p. 9; Sinhyu/Getty Images, p. 10; Juan Gärtner/Science Photo Library/Getty Images, pp. 11, 12; Shubhangi Ganeshrao Kene/Science Photo Library/Getty Images, p. 13; Kateryna Kon/Science Photo Library/Getty Images, p. 14; PIXOLOGICSTUDIO/Science Photo Library/Getty Images, pp. 15, 20; fcafotodigital/Getty Images, p. 16; LindaYolanda/Getty Images, p. 17; Hill Street Studios/Getty Images, p. 18; monkeybusinessimages/Getty Images, p. 19; Bymuratdeniz/Getty Images, p. 22; Dr Gopal Murti/Science Photo Library/Getty Images, p. 23; lenscap67/Getty Images, p. 24; Image Source/Getty Images, p. 25; Steve Gschmeissner/Science Photo Library/Getty Images, p. 26; Tom Merton/OJO Images/Getty Images, p. 27. Design elements: enot-poloskun/Getty Images (font); EduardHarkonen/Getty Images; atakan/Getty Images; kaylabutler/Getty Images; Eratel/Getty Images; gadost/Getty Images; Anastasiia_M/Getty Images; amtitus/Getty Images; desifoto/Getty Images; Yevhenii Dubinko/Getty Images; arthobbit/Getty Images; Freer/Shutterstock.com; cajoer/Getty Images; enjoynz/Getty; Benjamin_Lion/Getty Images. AR experiences: Hybrid Medical Animation.

Cover image: Sebastian Kaulitzki/Science Photo Library/Getty Images.

Lerner Publications Company
An imprint of Lerner Publishing Group, Inc.
241 First Avenue North
Minneapolis, MN 55401 USA

For reading levels and more information, look up this title at www.lernerbooks.com.

Main body text set in Aptifer Sans LT Pro.
Typeface provided by Linotype AG.

Designer: Kimberly Morales **Photo Editor:** Cynthia Zemlicka
Lerner team: Martha Kranes

Library of Congress Cataloging-in-Publication Data

Names: Leed, Percy — author.
Title: Guts (a stomach-turning augmented reality experience) / Percy Leed.
Description: Minneapolis : Lerner Publications, 2020. | Series: The gross human body in action | Includes bibliographical references and index. | Audience: Ages 8–11 | Audience: Grades 4–6 | Summary: "With closeup pictures and lots of disgusting facts, learn all about the gross science behind your body's digestive system."— Provided by publisher.
Identifiers: LCCN 2019041682 (print) | LCCN 2019041683 (ebook) | ISBN 9781541598065 (library binding) | ISBN 9781728401317 (ebook)
Subjects: LCSH: Digestive organs—Juvenile literature.
Classification: LCC QM301 .H88 2020 (print) | LCC QM301 (ebook) | DDC 612.3—dc23

LC record available at https://lccn.loc.gov/2019041682
LC ebook record available at https://lccn.loc.gov/2019041683

Manufactured in the United States of America
1-47997-48675-11/11/2019